Little Pink Pig

PAT HUTCHINS

Little Pink Pig

Red Fox

A Red Fox Book

Published by Random House Children's Books
20 Vauxhall Bridge Road, London SW1V 2SA

A division of Random House UK Ltd
London Melbourne Sydney Auckland
Johannesburg and agencies throughout the world

3 5 7 9 10 8 6 4

First published in the USA by Greenwillow Books 1994
First published in Great Britain by Julia MacRae 1994

Red Fox edition 1996

Printed in China

RANDOM HOUSE UK Limited Reg. No. 954009

ISBN 0 09 943291 9

For
Lucy Goundry

"Hurry up, Little Pink Pig," said Little Pink Pig's mother.
"It's time you were in bed."
"Wait for me," squealed Little Pink Pig.
 But Little Pink Pig's mother didn't hear him.

"OINK, OINK!" cried Little Pink Pig's mother.
"Where are you, Little Pink Pig?"
But Little Pink Pig couldn't hear her.

So Little Pink Pig's mother went to ask Horse
if he'd seen Little Pink Pig.
"Wait for me!" squealed Little Pink Pig.
But Little Pink Pig's mother didn't hear him.

"Have you seen Little Pink Pig?" she asked Horse.
"I've looked for him, and called for him,
 and it's time he was in bed."
 Horse looked, but he couldn't see him, either.
"**NEIGH!**" cried Horse. "Where are you,
 Little Pink Pig?"
 But Little Pink Pig couldn't hear him.
"Let's go and ask Cow if she's seen him," said Horse.

So off they went to look for Cow.
"Wait for me!" squealed Little Pink Pig.

But Horse and Little Pink Pig's mother didn't hear him.

"Have you seen Little Pink Pig?" they asked Cow.
"We've looked for him, and called for him,
and it's past his bedtime."
Cow looked, but she couldn't see him, either.
"**MOO!**" cried Cow. "Where are you, Little Pink Pig?"
But Little Pink Pig couldn't hear her.
"Let's go and ask the sheep if they've seen him," said Cow.

So off they went to find the sheep.
"Wait for me!" squealed Little Pink Pig.

But Little Pink Pig's mother and the horse and the cow didn't hear him.

"Have you seen Little Pink Pig?" they asked the sheep.
"We've looked for him, and called for him,
and it's past his bedtime."
The sheep looked for Little Pink Pig, but they couldn't
see him, either.
"BAA!" they cried. "Where are you, Little Pink Pig?"
But Little Pink Pig couldn't hear them.
"Let's go and ask the hens if they've seen him,"
said the sheep.

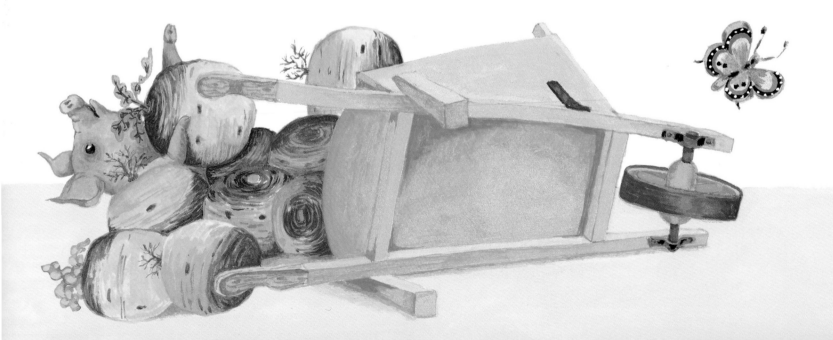

So off they went to find the hens.
"Wait for me!" squealed Little Pink Pig.

But Little Pink Pig's mother and the horse and the cow and the sheep didn't hear him.

"Have you seen Little Pink Pig?" they asked the hens.
"We've looked for him, and called for him,
and it's past his bedtime."
The hens looked for Little Pink Pig,
but they couldn't see him, either.
"CLUCK, CLUCK!" they called. "Where are you,
Little Pink Pig?"
But Little Pink Pig couldn't hear them.

Then Little Pink Pig's mother
and the horse
and the cow
and the sheep
and the hens all called together.

"OINK, OINK!"

"NEIGH, NEIGH!"

"MOO, MOO!"

"BAA, BAA!"

"CLUCK, CLUCK!"

"Where are you, Little Pink Pig?"

And this time Little Pink Pig heard them.
"Here I am," he said.

"Hurry up!" said Little Pink Pig's mother.
"It's past your bedtime."

"Wait for me!" squealed Little Pink Pig.